Danny came closer, closer, nearly touching it… then he jumped back as the half-drowned heap of fur exploded in the biggest sneeze Danny had ever heard. It sneezed and then it sneezed again. It sneezed itself right out of its wet heap until it was standing up on four legs with a brush of a tail hanging between its legs. It shook itself all over. Its wet fur flapped to and fro. It had a long nose and big eyes and sharp, pricked little ears. It shook the water off its fur and Danny saw that the fur was a red-brown colour, a bright warm colour, the colour of fire and autumn leaves and —

'Foxes,' said Danny.

The little fox looked straight at Danny and sneezed.

'Not ordinary fox,' he said. 'I'm Go Fox.'

Go Fox

GO FOX
A YOUNG CORGI BOOK : 0 552 52963 X
First publication in Great Britain by Young Corgi Books

PRINTING HISTORY
Young Corgi edition published 1996
Text copyright © Helen Dunmore 1996
Illustrations copyright © Colin Mier 1996

Set in Bembo Infant

Young Corgi Books are published by Transworld Publishers Ltd,
61-63 Uxbridge Road, Ealing, London W5 5SA,
in Australia by Transworld Publishers (Australia) Pty. Ltd,
25 Helles Avenue, Moorebank, NSW 2170,
and in New Zealand by Transworld Publishers (NZ) Ltd,
3 William Pickering Drive, Albany, Auckland.

Printed and bound in Great Britain by
Cox & Wyman Ltd, Reading, Berkshire

Go Fox

Helen Dunmore

Illustrated by
Colin Mier

YOUNG CORGI BOOKS

CONTENTS

'Go Fox! Go go go! Wow, Level Sixteen! I've never got past Level Twelve before. Go on, Go Fox! Go go go!' Danny crouched in front of the TV screen. His fingers on the controls flickered faster and faster. His eyes were fixed on Go Fox.

Go Fox raced under the tall
grey Spook Tree. The Spook
Tree moaned and reached down
spiky branches like skeleton
hands to grab Go Fox. Oh no!
Quick! Click! Quick! Go Fox
saw the skeleton hands just in
time. The branches of the Spook
Tree snapped shut like a cage
but Go Fox had escaped.

'Keep going, Go Fox! You've got to make it! Go go go, Go Fox!'

Suddenly Go Fox slid to a stop. Ahead of him was a raging river full of white foam, and rocks sharper than crocodiles' teeth. But Go Fox had to go on. Greedy green snappers were chasing him. Their jaws clashed as if they could taste Go Fox. They were coming closer.

One big snapper snapped his terrible fangs right on Go Fox's tail but Go Fox pulled his tail free. With a huge leap, Go Fox plunged into the wild river. Splosh! Water splashed up over the snappers and they leaped back. Snappers hate water and no snapper has ever learned to swim.

'Go Fox!'
shouted Danny,
'Get down deep in
the water, quick!'

Go Fox swam, but the river
was as fierce as the snappers.
Logs rushed and rolled down the
current. Go Fox swam for his
life but the logs rolled after him
like huge telephone poles. If
they hit him they would kill Go
Fox. One of the logs was as big
as a tree-trunk. It was going to
get him. Quick! Click! Quick!

Danny's fingers flickered on the controls, faster and faster. Go Fox dived and the log rolled by. He was safe this time. But now another log roared down the rapids to get Go Fox.

'Why can't you swim faster?' shouted Danny desperately. 'Go Fox! Go go go!'

14

Go Fox's big eyes stared straight at Danny as he swam for his life. And that's when Danny felt the first splash in his face. He blinked water out of his eyes. Click! Click! Click! He must keep Go Fox swimming. Splash! Another spray hit Danny's cheek like a cold slap. Then another.

Danny blinked and blinked again but the water ran in his eyes. He took his hand off the controls to wipe his eyes and he saw Go Fox swimming straight at him, as fast as he could go. Then another wave of icy water, the biggest yet, broke right in Danny's face and he shut his eyes.

CHAPTER TWO

When Danny opened his eyes again the TV screen was dark and blank.

'Oh no!' said Danny. 'All that water has wiped out my game!'

What would Mum say? What if the TV was broken?

'Mum's going to kill me,' moaned Danny. 'My computer game's bust and the TV's bust and there's water all over everything.'

But then Danny had an idea. If he dried the carpet quickly Mum would never know. He could blot up the water with kitchen towel, then put a big cushion on top of it. And maybe the TV would be all right. Danny looked down to see how wet the carpet was.

But there was something else
on the carpet. In the middle of
the patch of wet there was a
little browny-red heap of wet
fur, quite still. Danny stared at
it. Was it one of his baby sister's
teddies? No. None of her teddies
were that colour. Was it one of
next-door's ginger kittens? No.
It was more like a dog. A tiny
half-drowned dog.

Very, very slowly, not making a sound, Danny leaned forward and stared hard at the little half-drowned heap of wet fur. He came closer, closer, nearly touching it… Then he jumped back as the half-drowned heap of fur exploded in the biggest sneeze Danny had ever heard. It sneezed and then it sneezed again. It sneezed itself right out of its

wet heap until it was standing
up on four legs with a brush of
a tail hanging between its legs.
It shook itself all over. Its wet
fur flapped to and fro. It had a

long nose and big eyes and
sharp, pricked little ears. It
shook the water off its fur and
Danny saw that the fur was a
red-brown colour, a bright
warm colour, the colour of fire
and autumn leaves and—

'Foxes,' said Danny.

The little fox looked straight at Danny and sneezed.

'Not ordinary fox,' he said. 'I'm Go Fox.'

'Go Fox?' asked Danny in disbelief. 'You're Go Fox? Really Go Fox? But how did you get here?'

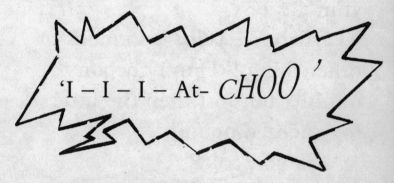

'I – I – I – At- *CHOO*'

sneezed Go Fox.

'You can't be,' whispered Danny. 'You just can't be. Go Fox isn't real. He's part of a computer game.'

But the little fox sniffed. 'Not real?' he said crossly. 'What do you mean, not real? I'm as real as you are. Realer. You're only the boy behind the glass.'

'The boy behind the glass?'

'Yes, that's right. Always staring in like a goldfish. You never do anything but stare, do you?'

'Of course I do. I do loads of other things!' Danny began angrily, but just then the little fox sneezed again.

'Are you cold?' asked Danny.

'Oh no! Not cold at all,' said the fox. 'Just sneezing for the fun of it. A – a – at – *CHOO!* Not cold in the very least. First those snappers, now this. I've had enough. This is the end. No more rivers for me. No more being chased and hiding and Spook Trees and snappers. No more running all the time. I've had enough.'

'Snappers? Spook Trees? Wow! So you really are Go Fox!' said Danny in amazement.

'Of course I am!' snapped
Go Fox. 'But I won't be for
much longer if I don't get dry.
I'll be Gone Fox.

A – a – at – *CHOOOO!*

'I'd better get you a cloth,'
said Danny. 'You wait here.
Danny ran to the kitchen
and grabbed a new roll of
kitchen towel. Luckily Mum
was upstairs changing his baby
sister's nappy. Danny tore off a
big wad of the towel and took
it back to Go Fox.

'Here you are,' he said, kneeling down on the wet carpet. 'Stand on this and I'll sort of pat you dry.'

'Sort of pat me dry?' said Go Fox. 'I'm not sure I like the sound of that. Just spread out that white cloth and I'll do the rest.'

So Danny spread the kitchen towel on a dry bit of carpet and Go Fox walked very very slowly and warily and stiff-leggedly over to stand in the middle of it. Go Fox tested the kitchen towel with his paws.

'Not bad,' he said. 'Not bad at all. In fact, almost perfect.'

Go Fox ducked down his head with its long nose and big bright eyes. He swished his big brush of a tail. He shook himself all over until drops of water spattered the kitchen towel. Then he tucked himself up into a ball and went head-over-heels. Over and over he went on the white sheets of super-strength kitchen towel, drying his red-brown fur. When he stopped, his fur was as soft and fluffy as a cloud.

'That's better,' said Go Fox. 'And to think I could still be swimming across that freezing cold river with logs the size of tower-blocks coming after me and you staring in like a goldfish. Now, would there happen to be anything to eat?'

'Hmm,' said Danny, thinking hard. 'I'm not sure. What do you like?'

'Oh, anything,' said Go Fox, watching Danny with bright, greedy eyes. 'Anything. You know. A plump little rabbit or two. Or a chicken. Would you happen to have a chicken?'

'Mum's got a frozen one in the freezer,' said Danny.

'Frozen! Brrr!' said Go Fox. 'I don't like the sound of that. Can't we go and catch a fresh one?'

'Well, no,' said Danny. 'There aren't any chickens round here, except in shops.'

'And no rabbits?'

'No. There's only
Mopsy next door. And
you can't have her.'

'What a pity,' said Go Fox,
licking his whiskers. 'What a
shame. Mopsy, did you say?
What a nice name. Perhaps I
could meet her some time.'

'I don't think so,' said Danny
firmly. 'What about a cheese
sandwich?'

'Cheese sandwich! Well, I
suppose so. If it's all you've
got,' said Go Fox.

Danny was good at making sandwiches. He put in plenty of cheese and some pickle and tomato. Go Fox walked all round the plate with the cheese sandwich on it. The sandwich looked enormous next to Go Fox.

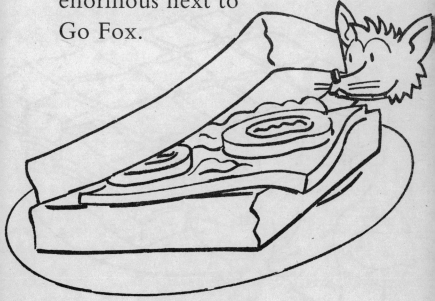

'Maybe I'd better cut it up,' said Danny.

'Yes. More fun that way,' agreed Go Fox. Danny cut up the sandwich into tiny squares on the plate. Go Fox crouched flat on his belly and started to slink up to the edge of the plate like a silent red shadow. Then he jumped. He pounced on a

square of cheese
sandwich and tossed
it high up in the air. As
it fell he snapped and
swallowed. He did it again and
again until all the cut-up
squares of cheese
sandwich were gone.
Then he licked his
whiskers.

'Why did
you do all
that
jumping?'
asked Danny
curiously.

'Oh, food's
no fun unless you
catch it yourself,
is it?' said Go Fox.

'How do you eat your food, then?'

Danny thought about what meals would be like if he and Mum and Dad and his baby sister all crept up to the table then jumped up in the air and snapped at their fish fingers and chips.

'Oh, we just eat it,' he said.

'Sounds boring,' said Go Fox. 'Don't you ever catch things? A nice plump little rabbit or a tasty fat hen?'

'No, we don't.'

'Oh, well,' said Go Fox. 'At least I'm dry. No nasty rivers here. Time for a sleep.'

And he curled up in the corner of a cushion, wrapped his tail around his body, put his head on his paws and fell asleep.

CHAPTER THREE

'Danny! DANNY!' called Mum.

'I'm watching TV!' shouted Danny.

'No you're not. You're playing that computer game. It's a lovely day and you ought to be outside. You can come to the park with me and the baby.'

'Oh, Mum! I'm busy,' said Danny, but then he heard Mum's footsteps coming closer. Quickly he threw his sweater over the cushion where Go Fox was sleeping.

'Good boy, you turned the TV off,' said Mum, standing at the door. 'Bring your sweater in case it gets cold.'

'All right, Mum, just coming.'

Danny bent down to pick up the sweater. As he did so he scooped up the soft fluffy ball of Go Fox into his hand and dropped it into his jeans' pocket.

But Go Fox woke in a second. Suddenly a dozen sharp needles pricked into Danny.

'Ow!'

'What's the matter, Danny?'

'Oh, it's OK, Mum. My foot hurt when I got up.'

'You've been sitting in front of that TV screen too long. Come here, I'll give it a rub.'

'It's all right now.'

On the way to the park, Danny pretended he had to stop to tie his trainers. As he bent down he whispered, 'You bit me! You bit me, Go Fox!'

Go Fox peered out of the top of Danny's pocket. 'Don't jog me up and down all the time,' he grumbled. 'I'm getting seasick in here. And I think there's bubble-gum on my fur. Bit you? That wasn't a bite. That was just a friendly nip. You should never pick up a fox when he's asleep.'

'Oh. All right, then. Sorry about the bubble-gum.'

'Danny!' called Mum from the park gates.

'Quick, get back in my pocket. We're nearly at the park. You'll like the park, Go Fox.'

But Go Fox didn't like the park. Danny couldn't go on the adventure playground with his friends because Go Fox was feeling sick again. Danny couldn't have a go on Jared's skateboard because Go Fox was afraid he'd get squashed if Danny fell off the skateboard.

But then Danny saw Mr Bailey's dog, Buster. Danny always threw sticks for Buster.

'Here, boy!' he shouted. 'Here, boy!' And he threw a stick way across the park. But Buster didn't run after it. Instead he came rushing up to Danny. He barked and jumped up at Danny. Danny saw all his teeth. He put his paws on Danny's legs and sniffed and whined. Then he opened his hot wide mouth.

'Help!' shouted Danny. 'He's going to bite me!

Help!' But Mum was a long way away, by the swings. Then Mr Bailey came running. 'Get down, Buster! Get down!' he shouted. Buster growled as Mr Bailey pulled him away by his collar. Danny felt shaky.

'I'm sorry,' said Mr Bailey.
'I don't know what's the matter
with him.' And he dragged
Buster away. Buster turned and
showed his teeth.

'Has he gone?' asked Go Fox
in a tiny voice. 'Has the
monster gone?'

'Yes, he's gone,'
said Danny.

'He was
trying to eat
me up with
his horrible monster teeth,' said
Go Fox. 'He could smell a poor
little fox in your pocket.'

'You're lucky. He nearly got
us,' said Danny. 'Are you all
right, Go Fox?'

'Let's go somewhere safe.
Let's go to your mum,' said Go
Fox.

'Oh, that's no fun,' said
Danny.

'Fun?' asked Go Fox bitterly.

'Fun? Do you think it's fun in your pocket, stuck to a big piece of bubble gum that's been in your mouth, being attacked by monsters?'

'No, I suppose not,' said Danny. 'Listen, do you like ice-cream? I'll ask Mum if I can have one.'

'Ice-cream!' said Go Fox. 'Yum. Ice-cream is good for foxes.'

Go Fox licked up nearly all the ice-cream and left the cornet for Danny.

'Very nice,' said Go Fox,

licking his whiskers. 'Ve-ry
nice. Ask her for another.'

'I can't do that. Mum never
buys me two ice-creams.'

'Why not?' asked Go Fox.
He went on asking 'Why not?'
for a long time, then he sulked
in the bottom of Danny's
pocket. Danny was glad when
Mum said it was time to go
home.

CHAPTER FOUR

'I'd better feed that baby,' said
Mum when they got home.
'You can watch TV for a bit
now, Danny.'

'OK, Mum.'

Mum didn't know the TV
wasn't working. She didn't
know about the water on the
carpet. She didn't know about
Go Fox. What if she found out?
Maybe Go Fox would know
what to do.

But Go Fox didn't. As soon

as he got out of Danny's pocket
he ran round and round the
carpet, shaking himself.

'That's better,' said Go Fox,
showing his sharp white teeth.
'I don't suppose you've got
anything I could chase?'

'No,' said Danny. 'Nothing.
Sorry, Go Fox.'

'Never mind,' said Go Fox with a big sigh. 'No juicy little rabbits. No plump hens. Just a whole lot of bubble gum.' And he sighed again.

'Are you hungry?'

'I'm always hungry,' said Go Fox, showing his teeth again.

'You could have some beans on toast. That's what Mum's making for me.'

'Beans on toast? BEANS ON TOAST! I'm not a vegetarian, you know.' And Go Fox showed his sharp white teeth again.

The TV screen was dark and blank. It would be nice to watch TV. It would be nice to play GO FOX.

'But how can I play GO FOX,' thought Danny, 'when Go Fox is here?'

He watched Go Fox running round and round the carpet, chasing his own tail. It looked very boring.

'Go on. You chase me,' said Go Fox.

'I'm too big. I might step on you. Anyway, you said you'd had enough of chasing.'

But Go Fox just ran faster and faster until he was a red-brown blur. Suddenly he stopped and lay still, panting.

'No tender little rabbits,' he panted. 'No melt-in-the-mouth chickens. Bubble-gum all over my beautiful fur. Monsters. And I'm still seasick from riding in your pockets.'

'You don't like it here, do you, Go Fox?' asked Danny sadly. Go Fox looked at Danny with bright dark eyes and shook his head.

'But where can you go? If I let you go a car might squash you.'

'Yuck! Don't talk about squashing! How can you live in such a dangerous place? Monsters in the park and cars that squash poor little foxes.'

'It's not dangerous. Not

really dangerous. Anyway,
where can you go?'

'Somewhere that's safer than
here,' said Go Fox. 'Turn on
the TV, Danny.'

'But it's broken.'

'Try. Turn it on. Then load
GO FOX.'

Danny touched the controls
and the TV switched on as if
there had never been anything
wrong with it. He plugged in
his games console and loaded
GO FOX. The game flashed up

on the screen just as it was
before. There was the raging
river. The snappers were still
on the river bank, snapping
their terrible fangs. But there
was no Go Fox swimming in
the water. No Go Fox at all.

'Brrr,' said Go Fox. 'That
water looks
freezing.'

'Stay here,
Go Fox,' said
Danny. 'You don't
have to go.'

'Look at those snappers! Bet they wish they could swim,' said Go Fox.

'What happens next?' asked Danny. 'What happens after you swim across the river?'

Go Fox stared at the screen. His nose pointed at the wild river. He trembled with excitement. 'I don't know what happens next,' he said, 'but I bet I get away. I bet I escape.'

'I bet you do, too,' said Danny.

'Thanks for the cheese sandwich,' said Go Fox politely.

'Sorry there weren't any rabbits,' said Danny.

'Oh, that's OK. Don't give it a thought.'

The river raged round the hungry rocks. Go Fox stared at the screen. His ears were pricked and his sharp white teeth shone.

'Go Fox –' began Danny,
but at that moment Go Fox
sprang like a red flame from a
fire, and the glass of the TV
screen parted for a second like
water to let him in. And he
was gone. Danny
jumped forward
to grab him, but
the TV glass was
solid again and
Go Fox was
gone.

Then Danny
saw something
swimming
hard in the white foam
of the raging river. A long wet
nose. A pair of bright dark
eyes. It was Go Fox! Go Fox,
swimming for his life. A huge
log tumbled down the rapids
towards him, but Go Fox saw
it before it hit him. He ducked
and dived, and as he came up
he looked straight at Danny.
One of Go Fox's bright dark
eyes shut for a second.

'He winked!' said Danny.
'Go Fox winked at me!'
Danny leaned forward,
staring at the screen. Level
Sixteen. What
came next? He
must find out
what happened
to his friend.
Would he swim
right across

the river? Would the logs get him? Would he be sucked down a whirlpool?

Just then Mum came in and put the baby down on the carpet beside Danny. 'Oh, Danny! Did you spill that lemonade I gave you?' asked Mum. 'This carpet's wet. Try and be more careful.'

'Sorry, Mum,' said Danny. He smiled. His fingers flickered on the controls, faster and faster. Click! Click! Click!

Danny stared at the screen
where a tiny red-brown fox
bobbed down the raging rapids.

'Go on, Go Fox!' whispered
Danny. 'Go go go!'

THE END